BE YOURSELF AND USE YOUR |
WITHIN YOU BECAUSE THE RIGHT PEOPLE WILL LOVE YOU

BE YOU
LOVE
YOU

Gershom Allen, DRG

FOREWORD BY THE SPIRIT OF LOVE AND PEACE

BE YOU LOVE YOU

Be You Love You

NAME: _____

DATE: _____

BE YOU LOVE YOU

ALSO BY GERSHOM ALLEN
The Perfect Love Triangle
Masterpiece
Victory
Dreams

"You are amazing"

BE YOU LOVE YOU

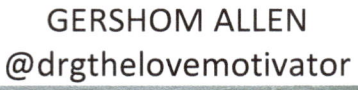

GERSHOM ALLEN
@drgthelovemotivator

BE YOU LOVE YOU

BE YOU LOVE YOU

BE YOURSELF AND USE YOUR POWER THAT IS WITHIN YOU BECAUSE THE RIGHT PEOPLE WILL LOVE YOU

GERSHOM ALLEN, DRG

LONDON ENGLAND
By way of Montserrat WI

BE YOU LOVE YOU

<u>DEDICATION</u>

I would like to dedicate this book to my wife and children, and to my mom and dad on their 46th years of wedding anniversary. To all the people around the world that have loved someone and forgot to love themselves first and who found the strength to overcome and fight through their adversities with all the pain inside.

****

BE YOU LOVE YOU

CONTENTS

Foreword by the spirit of Love and Peace

Introduction	Finding the Real You That Was Put in You
Chapter 1	You Can Only Be You, So Be You
Chapter 2	You Must Be Responsible for Your Actions
Chapter 3	You Can Only Be What You Believe You Are to Be
Chapter 4	You Must Find the Will to Heal Before You Love Fully
Chapter 5	Trust Yourself Before You Can Trust Anyone
Chapter 6	Embrace Your Failures Because You Are Only Human
Chapter 7	There Is No Growth Without Pain, To Build You, You Must Transform

BE YOU LOVE YOU

Chapter 8	Don't Settle for Less Than You Are Worth, It Will Kill You
Chapter 9	Your Self-Confidence and Self-Acceptance Is Your Salt and Sugar to Life
Chapter 10	Be You, Love You Because Everyone Else Is Taken
Chapter 11	Unconditional Love Is Everything to Live For, It Serves a Greater Purpose

ACKNOWLEDMENTS

ABOUT THE AUTHOR

AUTHOR PRAYER FOR YOU

The end.

INTRODUCTION

Finding The Real You That Was Put in You

The fact that you are holding this book in your hand and reading this right now is a sign that this book is for you. I wrote this very book thinking of you and to help you to understand who you really are.

You might think that this cannot be true, but the truth is I was right where you were some twelve years ago, to date, that I felt as if I was living a lie and I needed to find me. I know thousands of people might be reading this very same book, just like you, and you may think how do I know this is for you.

Let me say, I am speaking to you, right to you, because I know I wish that I had someone that would have done the same for me them years ago. The fact that you are reading this right now is that you are born and you are alive with

BE YOU LOVE YOU

understanding of knowing that life is for living. You have the gift of life and the power you have is endless if you are willing to take the journey of self-discovery. Yes! No one told me this is the part of life that will open to who you are and meant to be. This is called finding your true purpose.

If you are like me, a human, I can tell you that I have spent many of my years lost and confused of who I was to become and who I was meant to be. I did not understand why I was here and I know you may somehow feel that same way at times or if not, right now. I will help you, in this book, to give you some insight and understanding that I have learnt that has help me to become who I am and inspiring thousands of people every day.

How can I explain to you that many people said I would not come to anything and I was just a waste of time and I talk too much. I have spent so many years lost without knowing my true purpose and walking in my gift. This is what I will help you to understand and find.

I have been homeless and broken hearted that led me to suicidal thoughts with attempts. How could I be so lost and confused when I had the greatest gift one could have in my hands and wanted to give away? Life is everything and has such a wonderful power when you understand how loved you are and very important you are in this very moment in life's history. One thing that many of you have not done and have gone through life so far is not take time to get to know yourself and who you really are and not who others tell you that you are or who you should be. True love takes time and is by far the best thing that you will ever do when you decide to be and go as far as it can take you.

How could I, a collage dropout, become a self-published author, speaker and coach to thousands of people, with no handouts or support systems!? We are humans and we have the gift to create our own lives and not make excuses about what we don't have. It is very important to understand that life does not start with you or does not end with you. You are just a part of life and the circle of it. When I understood this, it opened my mind to see that I have the power to change and become whoever I think I can and want to be.

Right now, you must be very excited, just like me, that you are reading this book. I had just finished my new book called, "DREAMS" and I was sitting with my little girl, Eshani, and we were talking. She asked me a question. And I know you have asked yourself what made me start to write this book. I could not hold back and

BE YOU LOVE YOU

I know, that spirit, in the question, spoke to me and I had to respond very carefully. "Daddy, why don't everyone love each other?"

Yes, this is why you are reading this book right now because the answer to that question would help us to understand that it is important to love ourselves first in order to love others the way we should. God is love and love is God and when we love we become like God. Ok that's a mouthful for you and may take some time for you to receive. You will find that as you read this book you will see that you can only be you and not be who everyone wants you to be. That's why, as you grow and get older, your friends and family change around you and can make you get so upset with yourself that you can become so broken and lost.

I can tell you that I have been living my life for twelve years and I have been on this planet for 40 years. Every day, since my awakening, I have been reaching towards my highest potential. I have been speaking all over the world in schools, colleges and universities. I had my own masterminds and coaching classes. I have been helping people to live their best life and to walk into their greatness every day. So, if you have just found me, this should be amazing for you and if you have been one that has been walking with me,

BE YOU LOVE YOU

step by step, lets continue to grow and become as amazing as we can together.

BE YOU LOVE YOU

BE YOU
LOVE YOU

Affirmation

******

I am at the right place at the right moment.
Everything is right where it should be.
Today I will do what is right for me and take care of myself. I will take full responsibility of my time and go where I need to be. Everything I want is coming to me. I have everything I need.
Nothing will stop me from doing the right things for me so I can be who I really want to be.
I will take time to learn what I don't know. I will not be afraid to ask for help so that I will improve my skills to better me. I will be me and love me because I am valuable.

BE YOU LOVE YOU

CHAPTER 1
YOU CAN ONLY BE YOU

Take control of what you can control even when things seem out of control and you will soon see that you are in control.

You can only be you may sound very obvious, but the truth is that many people have lost themselves so much that they don't really know who they are and are upset with who they are becoming every day and don't know how to change it. Have you ever found yourself in a conversation with a family member or close friend and you just seem to be agreeing with everything they say? And when you walk away, from the conversion, you ask yourself, why did you not speak you mind and your thoughts about something?

Well, I have been there and I had to unlearn this and to be able to speak my truth at all times or not say anything at all. I could remember me speaking with my father and mother about me not staying in London anymore because it was not where I wanted to be. They were very upset and disappointed that I did not want to be near them anymore. This by far was one of the hardest conversions I have had, but by far the best one ever as I really found my voice and my truth to who I was. That's where it all started for me.

You see, you may have become a person that doesn't want to upset anyone or just doesn't like the uncomfortable feeling when your truth is making someone else uncomfortable. This, I have learned, is called growth outside of you. The moment you learn that you are always growing and learning, is the moment, you start really living to who you really are. It will take you some time to unlearn this behaviour, but once you have you will soon see that you are better off always speaking your truth or not say anything at all.

Knowing when to take the leave is very important to know what you can and can't take. It's not everything that you need to be a part of even if you think that you are going to be alone. The truth is you are never alone. Stop letting other people put their truth on you and believing it.

I could remember walking miles to school as a little boy on the island of Montserrat after going to look after the animals and doing some gardening at times. Just having boiled sweet potatoes and a cup of bush tea, with a promise of

BE YOU LOVE YOU

lunch that my dad would bring at lunch time, it was not easy at all. And it felt so uncomfortable at times because I would see the other children with their packed lunches and I would not have any.

Coming from a very humble, poor family I can tell you that some people in the community would sometimes look down upon us as a family, but I knew that my father and mother were doing their best. Not wanting to believe or accept this truth could have made me do wrong things to have things that I could not afford, but knowing who I was kept me on at right part. You may be living like this, not wanting to live within your means and living outside of it, and this is not your truth and it will push you to be someone that you are not.

There could only be one you and this is what you must believe and understand. No matter how many people are in this world, you are the only one of a kind that is here with the chance to do what you can do to create in this world. You must embrace you in order for you to live a life that is full. Stop looking at everyone around you and focus on you. Yes, focus on you. Have you really done this? Be truthful. Where your focus goes your energy flows. You have the power to be whoever you want to be.

BE YOU LOVE YOU

You have heard the saying that people can be a product of their environment? Well, this is true if you don't take time to know who you are created to be. Yes! I said who you are created to be. We all have something that we enjoy to do and fully come into our true self when we are doing this thing. You see, in order for you to be who you truly are, you must be willing to not let anything stop you from being. We are always learning and growing into our full self. There is not a situation that we have come up against that was not meant to be for us. Yes, the good and the bad. You have a story and your story might be close to someone else, but it would never be the same to them.

You are beautiful and the only, one of kind. You have the power to be the first and the only one. You can stand alone and be like the sun. There many other stars that shine, but none like you. It's your choice to shine as bright as you want to, so just be you. You have that talk with yourself every day and say the things that you don't think you can tell anyone else and just remember this world is not going to be the same without you.

Affirmation

✶✶✶✶✶✶

I have the courage to learn something new today. I will use the courage I have to overcome my fears today. I am strong enough to stand up
for myself because I am never alone for, I know that God is with me, at all times. I will embrace my tough times because I know that my tough times are what make strong times. I know that in the moment of my tough time is what makes me appreciate the good time even more. I know good things are coming for me and my tough days don't last so I will continue to have a positive attitude today and every day that comes.

_____

BE YOU LOVE YOU

CHAPTER 2
You Must Be Responsible For Your Actions

When you think everything is some's fault, you will suffer a lot. When realize that everything springs only from yourself, you will learn both peace and joy. - Jim Rohn

All my life, I can tell you that this was at lesson my father and mother have tried their best to teach me because they believe that God had something great for me to do. My father's been an active Elder in the church and I could never understand where he got the strength or the energy to keep going and be in charge of opening and closing up the church as he had be the first two be there and last to leave. And now to think about it, he also had the responsibility to open and close up the school where he worked for most of his life and me and my brothers and sisters had to be there every step to help him this was our responsibility. We did not have a choice in that and it was very hard for us as the other children would laugh at us at times. It was the only other high school on the island everyone as we went to the seventh day Adventist school that was the other high school. My father and mother believed in putting God first in everything that we do and it's something that I have put in my life because this is what has help me to be who I have become.

    Yes, my father was very responsible and I too want to be like him. Being in a big family, a family of eight, you can get lost with falling behind with the things that you had to complete before the sun came up and the sun went down. It seems as if there were not a lot of hours in the day. Hearing my father singing and his hands going, making mats, at the same time and mom in the kitchen making breakfast, you knew it was time to get up and worship and give God thanks, as a family, for the new day. You did not want to be awakened with the footsteps of my dad coming with the belt to wake you or, on the other hand, the grace of a mother that would tell you, you must get up as you father is ready. You knew this was the first most responsible thing that had to take place of every new day. So, if you would say that this would be hard for 0…5, 6, 7, 8… year old, my father believes that early to bed early to rise makes a man healthy, wealthy and wise. Then the task for the day was set out and was given to every child and had to be completed

BE YOU LOVE YOU

before the end of the day. Some would say that life can be unfair or hard but I have learned that life is what you think about that most. I did not really care much about how hard things where in my home that I grow up because we were mostly hard and hard peace in our home. Love was always there and it was our escape from the tuff life that we had.

Your love is your first responsibility and yes this might sound simple but it is true. It is everything that you must first become the master of. I will tell you that once you are able love truly the way you should you will understand that everything else will come. Ok how do you love yourself truly is the big question. Well it starts with loving God and your creator and taking time to understand who is because you are his child so you are truth of who you are in found in Him. Your I am is His I am that has the power two call the this you want and need to you. If you are full then you are able to be truly happy. Your happiness is your responsibility. Yes, it is and it's not you mom or dad once you have come two have understanding that it's not your boyfriend, girlfriend, husband or wife... or anyone that you think should make you happy. Once you start two take full ownership of your life you will find that you can be whoever you want to become or have

BE YOU LOVE YOU

all that you really way to make you happy. You owe yourself that much. You have the strength to make more in this life no matter situation you are born in to. I can tell you watching my parents live their life together has shown me the beauty of life and living in love. Even when you lose everything and you have zero. I have learned that zero is at number and it's never to be over look. Even if you don't seem two have you have everything because everything starts with a word. If you can speak it that you can have it. Take full responsibility of everything you do and you will see that you will start become more respected. Yes, this is what makes you grow. Life is about movement and if you are not growing then you are nothing truly living. Don't be trap in feelings and letting control your outcome. Feelings can change like the weather. Yes, you must live at life of principles if you want to get result.

BE YOU LOVE YOU

Affirmation

★ ★ ★ ★ ★

Today I will open my heart for love and to show love to someone new. I will be kind to everyone I meet and to a stranger. I choose to make someone happy with my smile because it's free. I will not forget to say I am sorry. I have a kind heart to everyone. I will open my heart to enjoy the day and what it brings. I will love every moment of today. I will be happy, come what may, and always remember too that today could be my last day. I am ready to do my best in every second of this day, come what may. I am strong on this glorious new day. I will be me and love me
every single day.

———————

CHAPTER 3
You Can Only Be What You Believe You Are to Be

To be or not to be, this is the question that we should all answer in order to have the life that we truly want to live. In every moment of life, we are becoming even if we choose to or not for with the movement of time is the grace of growth. – Author words

Once I heard a story of how an eagle's egg somehow got put with a chicken and did not know that he was not a chicken. When he hatched, he lived and grew with the chicken for most of his life. Every day he would be getting bigger and bigger. The other chicken would look at him funny and laugh at him. They did not really understand he was so different and act so different. The eagle did not know he was an eagle and was broken and confused that he was so different. When they were eating together, there was a problem. When they were working together, he found it difficult to do. He just did not feel as if he could fit in. One day, he saw some other eagle, that looked just like him, flying very high up in the sky and he said that he looks the same. He went and asked the mother hen, "Why do I look like the eagle that is flying up above so high?" His mom explained to him what had happened and how the farmer put his egg with her and she had taken care of him till now. In that moment, the eagle had believed that he was a chicken for so long.

You may find this very funny or it may just be a joke, but the truth is many of us believe that we are something we are not because things that your family or people that have come into your life may have told you, you are. And you have tried your best to fit in when really you were meant to stand out and be you. Yes, be you and whoever you know and think you should be.

I could remember me getting exams and seeing 15% out of 100% with a big red fail at the end of it and then to be told by my teacher that, "Your head is too hard to learn." Somehow, I was believing them. I was becoming that child that could not spell, read or write. Well, right up to adulthood, well, around the age of 25, 26… I did not think that I could learn. I think that I was just dunce like they called me. It took time for me to unlearn this mind-set and the only way I could have done so was by loving myself.

BE YOU LOVE YOU

****

SOMETIMES YOUR PLSNS DON'T WORK OUT BECAUSE GOD HAS BETTER ONE FOR YOU

****

BE YOU LOVE YOU

You become what you believe and this is what you must understand about you. You must believe in yourself no matter what anyone thinks and says about you. Speak words of positivity into your life every day.

With every new morning, start with a prayer of thanks and total gratitude for who you are and where you have come from. Everything that you are in or going through is to bring out the better in you. As a man think, so is he. Yes, I know you have heard this time and time before. Though, the truth is, do you really believe it?

Everything starts with one thought. It's for you to think it so you can bring it to life. You have the power of God in you. You are, every moment of your life, creating something that you need and desire. Your belief is where all your best life is! And I know you can see the nice car, the house, the money and everything else that you want. If you can see it, you can have it and you thinking about it brings it to life!

The truth is what you do next with your thoughts is what pushes your thoughts away or

BE YOU LOVE YOU

brings your thoughts close to you. You ever try to think about more than one thing at a time? Have you ever thought, why you cannot think about more, though, at a time? Well, I know it's because everything comes into life with order. That's why some people still can't answer the question, what comes first that chicken or the egg? Well, if you don't know the answer, then your faith needs to be really thought about more.

You see, I know it's the chicken because I know I was created so that I can create and this is really the truth about life. We are constantly creating our lives. Your thoughts are creating your life every second. And if you don't know what comes first, if it's the chicken or the egg, then you are really in a bad place because you are living in doubt. You know that doubt is the number one thing that kills more dreams than anything else.

It's time for you take full control of your thoughts and what you truly believe and this will change your life and the results you are getting every day. Have you ever thought about getting a red car and then when you start looking for the red car you seem to see a red car everywhere you go more often than before? Well, that's because you are looking with your thoughts and bringing it into your focus.

BE YOU LOVE YOU

It was youth camp that my parents said we had to go to and I did not really want go because I had a problem; yes, that problem, I was wetting my bed into my late teens. At the time, I did not know what I was going to do; I was going to be embarrassed. I went to the camp. It was early morning; I woke up and I was wet. I was feeling terrible and I did not know what to do. I knew all my friends would find out and it would be the worst for me.

This is when it happened that I started to change my thoughts about me not being seen or even wetting myself and yes, I did not. I found my power of my thoughts and what I believe in that moment. Later on, I found out, from seeing a sociologist, that this was all a part of my learning disability, later on in my life.

You see, your belief is very important to the results you get in your life; it connects to your instinct. The clearer you are with your thoughts, the better results you get with what you want in this life. Just be yourself at every time of your life. Be true to who you are. Remember that it's your life and your belief that makes your life what is it. Be you, love you.

BE YOU LOVE YOU

Affirmation
★★★★★

I am enough. I am a masterpiece. I am a gift. I am loved. I am powerful. I am amazing. I have the solution to the problem. I will make it through my pain. I am able to transform. I am success. I am happy. I am at peace with who I am. I am who God created me to be. I am royalty.

———————

CHAPTER 4

You Must Find the Will to Heal Before You Love Fully

Healing is an art. It takes lots of work. It takes practice. It takes a willing person to listen to their heart and soul. It takes love. Forgiveness is the door to true love that lasts forever. — Author words

One day I was sitting by the sea side, watching the waves come in. I started to throw stones into the water trying to make them bounce on the water. I could see a young lady crying and standing in the water. I called to her asking if she was ok. I was worried for her as the water was getting rough. The waters were getting high. I got as close as I could to see if I could help and asked what was the problem. She opened her mouth and said to me in a loud voice, "Life is unfair." As I got close to her, I asked her to take my hand and walked together out of the water. I asked her to tell me why life is so unfair. She told me that things where just not going her way for love and every time she gives her heart to someone, they would just break it over and over again.

That was a true story, and I will tell you what I told her that life is not meant to be fair in order to get the best out of life. This life will be full of pain and hurt until that last breathe of air in our lungs. You may ask why I say this, so let me say it this way. It's not fair that woman should go through pain to bring life into this world. It's not fair that some babies never make it to see their first birthday and it's not fair that some people have a lot of money and others do not.

Well, this is the world we live in and until you are willing to accept this, you will not be able to heal fully. That's right. There are many of things that are happening around us every day and it affects the way we look at others and how we make our choices from day to day. In many ways, this can be very painful to our heart that we have become so numb to how we choose to love others as we love ourselves.

We should all take time to look at ourselves and who we really are and understand what we want of this life. Healing is a daily process. It is constant forgiving spirit that flows through you to others and not holding onto pain that you can't

BE YOU LOVE YOU

control. Sadly, pain is a part of this life and will be until you leave it. Take time to meditate and pray; it's very important to upstanding the power of love that you have that you can use to bring things into your life that you want.

Our families can be some of our biggest problems to ever really having love or giving love to others. Some would say that some people prefer to show love to animals more than they show love to humans because they can't hurt them the way humans do. You will have to find the strength to let go of what you can't control and control the things you can. Never try to not be you and love you because of other peoples' hurt and pain that they try to put on you.

To fully love, you must be willing to fully let go. Yes, total freedom. This is hard to do for many as they don't have no control over what could happen and fear can come into play.

Affirmation

★ ★ ★ ★ ★

I will trust the road and where it is taking me. I believe that God knows what's best for me. I will use everything I have to its fullest. I will make the adjustments that I need to get everything out of every day. I will choose to be all I can be. I will trust that who I becoming is what God wants me to be. The world needs me and I am important to the world. I will have the faith to believe that everything is working for me. My life is beautiful. I will make the plans I need, to be who I need to be, for my dreams. I will love me and trust me in all that I do. I will just be me.

_____

CHAPTER 5
Trust Yourself Before You Can Trust Anyone

BE YOU LOVE YOU

The most important lesson that I have learned is to trust God in every circumstance. Lots of times we go through different trials and following God's plan seems like it doesn't make sense at all. God is always in control and He will never leave us.
                                    Allyson Felix

I was about 9 years old, at the time, and we were all excited to go to the seaside. We had already done all our work for the day and my dad said, "Let's all get into the car and let's go to a church outing at the seaside." I was excited as I love being in the water and just to be around water. That day a lot of people were there, I could remember. It was lots of fun. We played games and had lots to eat. I was having a lot of fun with my friends, but the only thing was I was not a strong swimmer. I could remember asking and getting a tube to float with on the water. I was laying on it, out in the water, like at boat on the sea. It was so much fun. Then my brother Noel and his friend came and took the tube from me. All I could remember is me starting to go down, my feet could not touch the ground. Every breathe I took I was swallowing water. I could not see anyone and I just could see the light shining through. I was screaming for help but no one seemed to hear me. Then I felt a hand grab me and the next thing I knew was I was coughing up water laying on the sand. That day I knew that I came closer to God because I knew he heard my voice and allowed me to be alive.

    That day everything changed for me. I knew that there was a higher power and that if I cry out that He knew my voice. And I had to trust that He would come through for me. I am not telling you to believe in God or to find a religion. I am just telling you that I found that someone greater than any human heard my voice and came to me.

    Now this is the hard part of life. Can you trust that things will work out for when you can't see it and it don't make sense? You see, you don't even know how to trust yourself anymore so how can you trust people? You have to learn how to trust yourself all over again, that you know what you want and to make the right choices that are best for you.

Your instinct is always right and this is the truth. You will have to learn how to connect to it and trust that it will lead you to what is best for you. You may have been betrayed by people you love and this has got you broken, but the only way you are going to be able to have the life you want is if you are able to let go of that and forgive yourself.

For you to love you, you must trust you totally. Yes, trust your failure and your success, that it will all be worth it and take you to where you are meant to be. You are the only one of kind and no one can be you and do you. You are enough. You are choosing to live in this time and be all you can be. Yes, you can do all you can dream of, but you must trust yourself.

BE YOU LOVE YOU

✶✶✶✶✶

Trust in the LORD with all thine heart; and lean not unto thine own understanding. In all your ways acknowledge Him, And He shall direct your paths.

Proverbs 3:5-6

Affirmation

★★★★★

Yesterday does not define me. I will not live in the past. I will live in my now and do my best to make me at my best. I will write my own story. I will become the master of what I want. I will be true to me. I will fill myself up first so that I can pour from my overflow. Life is what I make it and I will make it my best life. I will get out of my own way. I will stay true to my word because my word is important. I will be trustable. I will be the one to be the first to trust that I will make it to my dreams. I will believe in my dreams. I will be me and love me.

_____

CHAPTER 6

Embrace Your Failures Because You Are Only Human

BE YOU LOVE YOU

Many times what we perceive as an error or failure is actually a gift. And eventually we find that lessons learned from that discouraging experience prove to be of great worth. — Richelle E. Goodrich

"Son don't follow your mind this morning," were the words you would hear from my dad about 5am to his 10- and 8-years old sons. "We got to go now." It was cold and dark and we had to go out into the morning before we go to school that morning. My father was a very hard-working man and always seemed to be busy. He would say, "the devil finds work for idle hands, so we are to make sure that our hands are busy doing something constructive at all times." If it was not in the garden or house duties, it would be reading the bible or doing school work. You see life growing in the village of Windy Hill, Montserrat was full of tasks set for the day and they all had to be completed by the end of day. How could I not tell you about taking care of the animals. Remember if they don't eat, you don't eat. We had sheep and goats; oh, we had a donkey too. Life was fun but very busy with no time to waste. My father was a strong believer in doing your best and giving your best at all times no matter what. Don't make excuses about what you can't get done. Where there is a will, there is a way. Some would say I am somewhat like him and my wife would keep telling this over the years that I always seem to find a way.

There is no failing with my father because he does not know how to quit. I call him the fighter. You see coming from little or nothing to eat some days, but a pray for a miracle, mom would just put on the fire and somehow a neighbour would turn up with a bag of food. I have seen this happen so many times in our house that's why my faith is what has guided me so far on this journey to inspire the world with my story.

Learn from your failure and you will never fail if you try again until you succeed. Many people say that failure is hard, but I have learned that failure is the greatest lesson if you just applied what it taught you. And know, that is a

BE YOU LOVE YOU

way not to do it and you just got to find the way to get it done.

Who tells you that failure was such a bad thing? Well, for me I have learned in order for me to get better and be better I must be willing to go after it no matter what and that my failures are always trying to teach me something. It's building my strength and my courage to keep going. I just would keep becoming stronger and stronger every time.

Could you image, if the slaves had not embraced their failures and they quit, what this world would have been like? You see no human is perfect. This is what you must believe and always remember, but there are those who know how to hide and cover up better than others. Love your failures and take them with a smile because it is making you into what you want to become and making you that much better than the person that you were before the failure.

Remember we are just humans, are just dust and air. Yes, this is true. The only thing that makes us special is what we do for others and the things that we leave better for others after we are gone. You have to make the choice of who you will be and who you will want to be remembered to be.

BE YOU LOVE YOU

The truth is your life can change at any time so don't waste your time focusing on what you can't do and focus on what you can do. And your failures show you what you can do. Just become a master of that and you will be able do more after you master what you can do.

This is my fifth book and I can't tell you how I am doing this because I could not spell, read, write or type at the age of 27 and I had to push myself because I wanted to become a master of helping with my story. I watch all the great speakers with books like Les Brown and I had to find a way to do it. But most of all, I just wanted to help you, yes you, and I am telling you if I can, so can you. So, I just keep failing my way here. I think your failures are more valuable than your success, but it's for you to pay close attention to what it is trying to teach you.

BE YOU LOVE YOU

Affirmation

*****

I am the only one of me. I will not be doubting myself. I will give myself a chance to try. I will never give up on me. I will take on the challenge to be more than I am. I will push myself. I am winning. I am a champion. Today I will complete my task for the day. I will never ever give up on myself. I will do my best at all times. I will never fail because I will never quit. I am a blessing to others. I will deal with my problems. I will always give myself the grace that I give others.

_____

CHAPTER 7
There is No Growth Without Pain, Build You, You Must Transform

BE YOU LOVE YOU

Growth is painful. Change is painful. But nothing is as painful as staying stuck somewhere you don't belong. - Mandy Hale

What is your deepest fear? This is one of the hardest questions to answer for a lot of people. Well, I know that many people are fearful of not having the life that they want. You can only control yourself and you should always remember that. Many people will never understand the power they have when they choose to take full control. The truth is you have the power to transform your life at any time. Fear makes a lot of people stuck and not able to move from where they are. This could be one of the deepest fears ever.

The fear of change. The truth is without change nothing improves. A baby does not stay a baby forever. As times fly by, they grow and become an adult. Everything in this life changes in time. One thing I know for sure is that pain comes with growth and change. Life will give you things that you never expect to happen to you. All pain is temporary. Pain has a way of talking to you; it is telling you that something is changing, something new is giving birth. Many people want a new thing to happen in their life, but they don't want to go through pain.

When I was going through my brokenness of a broken heart it is what started me on this purpose. Yes, after dating a young lady for six and half years then asking her to marry me, she said to me that she wanted, "to be as free as a bird." I lost myself totally. I fell into a deep depression. If I tell you, that is by far the best thing that has happened to me, you would not believe me.

I was listening to the story that I told myself that others told me. My teachers and other people said that I was hard headed, a dunce and I would never become anything. At that low point, all I wanted to do was to be alone and not talk to no one. I felt lost, but not knowing that I was getting to know who I was all over again. I had to start loving myself and value who I was. This was painful, but eye opening and transforming.

Yes, I cried out to God and I was struggling with the thoughts of taking my own life. I did not want to be here. I hit rock bottom and it was painful. Then I heard the voice of God say to me…....PUSH … PUSH GERSHOM. I could feel the change coming, but with tears coming out of my eyes I managed to roll out of bed and start to do some push ups and yes, the next words I heard changed myself forever PUSH PAST THE PAIN GREATNESS IS NEXT.

Yes, I did push every day. I started to take care of my body, running, going for long walks and helping others to heal from their brokenness. And that has led me to writing this book, my 5th book, and traveling the world helping thousands of people to live their best life every day.

Would you believe that I thank God for breaking me so that He can make me into who He wants me to be? I could not see me being no one else than I am today and I am truly grateful that I embrace my pain. You might be or have gone through pain of some kind that you are hurting right now and you found me or my book and it's not by chance it was made for you too so that I can help you and so you can transform in this time of your life to live out your true purpose.

This is your time to build something much bigger than you. You go to a place where loving you can only take you, right to the heart of God. Yes, He is in you and gave you a gift and dream for you to live a wonderful life better than you are living and to be the light for others.

BE YOU LOVE YOU

Yes, start to build with faith and stop thinking about the how. That is not up to you. Faith is hearing His voice and following his will, not your will but His will. And all the rest, the blessing will come like a rushing win and all the abundance will come with it.

I have never known a king or queen to not have a kingdom. It comes with it. Faith and trusting that His plan for you is greater than you ever had. It will open you to the best life you could ever image. It's just for you to do the work every day.

Stop looking at what is gone and believe that he will restore and rebuild something new and amazing with your pain. You will become the seed that was buried from His creation of you long before your pain came to wake you up to better and bigger plans for you. He wants you to expose you to a new life and to give you more than you can imagine. Build it.

Affirmation
★★★★★★

Today is the perfect day. It is the best day to do amazing things. Today is a great day for me to be all I can be. Today is a beautiful day. Today is a peaceful day and I am at peace. Today my spirit is full of joy and happiness. Today is a perfect day. Today I focus on me and the beauty that is in me. I am full of love and wealth of overflowing gratitude. I will make the best of this perfect day. I am perfect because God made me so. I am loved by God as His only child. I know I am never alone. I will be the light for others to see. I will be the shoulder for others to cry on for I am strong. My heart is healed from pain and hurt. I will never let yesterday's pain define me. I will let my pain refine me into who God wants me to be. I will use it to help others and to make others strong. I am so blessed by His mercy.

BE YOU LOVE YOU

BE YOU LOVE YOU
NO MATTER WHAT

BE YOU LOVE YOU

CHAPTER 8

Don't Settle for Less Than You Are Worth It Will Kill You

BE YOU LOVE YOU

You have to learn to love yourself before you can love someone else. Because it's only when we love ourselves that we feel worthy of someone else's love.

You are what you choose. Yes, that's right you can only be as you think you are and what you choose. You must be the one that makes the choice for you. Many people let other people make some choice for them and they are not happy with the choice.

I remember it was a few months into dating my now wife and I was thinking of asking her to be my wife. I asked one of my brothers this question of what do you think and what I should do because there was some situation coming up with another woman making it clear that she was the better woman for me. So, I asked for advice from my bother. He said what he would do and then said to me, "The choice is yours!" And I said,

BE YOU LOVE YOU

"You did not help me. You told me all you think, but you did not tell me what you would do." I felt like it was by far the best thing he could have done for me. If he did say this one or that one, I would have said it was his fault.

This is your life and no one could really live your life for you. You must make the choices yourself for what you want. Don't let anyone make them for you. You must know who you are and if you don't know, then you should take the time to get to know who you are, now. Many people settle for less and then live the saddest life ever.

In order to be you, you must take full control of you. This may sound simple, but it is the key to having everything you want and in order to be you and love you. The number one thing that you must master is how you use and control your time. It is by far one of our biggest things that you would ever be happy to know that you have mastered it.

We all have 24 hours in a day. Ok, it took me 9 days to write this book and you would say no way as I work 50 hours one week, 40 the next, I am father and I have a life of an entrepreneur. So, you would ask how I did it. Well, while my wife and kids are sleeping, I am up working on it. So, I had to lose sleep to make this happen.

BE YOU LOVE YOU

Time is what you do with it that makes it count and how you choose to take action. I go to the gym and I spend 40 minutes and put in the work and I get the results I am looking for. Then I see others go to the gym; they spend 2, 3, 4 hours and they don't get the results because they spend time talking, looking in the mirror and on their phone.

You see, the truth is your focus level is important to the results you have. Stop wasting time on doing the things that will not get you the result you want. Become in full control of every second of your time and you will start to see that you will start to win more in your life. Stop focusing on things you can't control and on wasted conversation. The more time conscious you become is the more, you will soon see, you become even more valuable. People with think before they come to try and waste your time.

This is killing a lot of people these days. They spend a lot of their time just scrolling through their phones for hours and just watch their life past them by. They are just getting closer to their expiry date. When you understand your value then other people will value you and if they don't, then don't give them your time. You're the prize and you are worth every second that you give away to anyone. The time glass with the sand is always running out and you and having less time to live out your passion and dreams if you waste your time.

When you know what you are worth then you should go and get what you are worth. You can choose to be the star or the sun, the one that others get their light from or be the one that is reflecting the light from others. I like to be the light for others and to help others to become the light.

BE YOU LOVE YOU

Affirmation

★ ★ ★ ★ ★

I will trust myself fully and totally. I will have self-confidence and self-acceptance. I will value who I am because I am more valuable than money. I will make room for more and wealth that God has for me. I don't need anyone to approve me. I know that I am already approved and I am just going to be me. I am like the wind when I enter the room you will feel me before you see me. Everything that the enemy throws at me I am strong and will deal with it because God will turn it around for me. I will sing a new song today for I am coming out a champion. I am to go to the next level. I will Be Me and love me.

———————

CHAPTER 9

Your Self-Confidence and Self-Acceptance is Your Salt and Sugar to Life

Confidence is your beauty and strength that God has put inside of you. Your beauty is not meant to be hidden, but to be seen, the light that you are. When you truly accept who you are, you will soon see that you will attract what you need to live out a full life.

    I know that you may think that your life no one really understands or no one really listens to you at all. You may feel a bit lost and out of touch. The truth is that life will want you to be confident in you and to know who you are is who you are. No one can really tell you who you are. It's up to you to really stand up and speak up. Be bold and confident because no one can really do this for you, but you.

    Finding your own voice can be hard if you have lost your voice while you're going through some traumatic situation. Life is about community and sometimes our communities let us down. Right down to our families who we expected to be there for us, but did not. And to top it off, they were a part of it because they saw what you are going through or what happened and they did nothing. Then you fall into the blame game where you blame everyone for what went wrong or is going wrong.

When I was young, I attended Pathfinder's Club. It was where I learned a lot of life skills that help me today. We would do drills and fall in straight lines from the tallest to the shortest. It was not easy. The worst thing was, I would be at the end of the line most or if not, all the time. The part that I hated was the numbering off. I would have to shout out my number because I was at the end of the line most times. I could remember that the other children would laugh at me because of how I sounded and make fun of it.

The truth is, as time went on, and being on parade days, I grew more and more confident that I could remember being at the Queen's birthday parade and the Governor stopped to talk to me and said "Young man, how old are you?" I said, "I am 9 years old sir." He then said this. "You have done yourself proud today." The spotlight was on me. If you could see my smile. That moment everyone was looking at me. You could see me wearing my confidence. Since that day I have learned to never

BE YOU LOVE YOU

feel embarrassed about being confident because someone is always watching. At the right time, it would put you in the right spotlight.

Be who you are, at all times, no matter what. You can only be you and no one else. You only look good wearing you. No matter who you look up to or respect someone, you have the same power of them when you accept you and be you. You could be inspired by someone or motivated, but you can never be happy to live a great life being someone else.

When you are making at exotic drink it would never be as good without sugar. Confidence is your sugar to life; it makes who you are stand out from the rest. Don't let anyone make you feel less than you are. Wear your confidence with a smile.

BE YOU LOVE YOU

******

For the foolishness of God is wiser than human wisdom, and the weakness of God is stronger than human strength.

Note: Nothing that you are going through is ever wasted.

BE YOU LOVE YOU

Affirmation

★ ★ ★ ★ ★

Today I will challenge myself every day to be better than I was yesterday. I will push past my pain to get to my greatness. I have the ability to overcome any of life challenges that come my way. My life is full of abundance and joy and full of grace. I will become successful with anything that I do. I have the strength to rise up from my pain and hurt. I will work hard and be smart at the same time for what I want. I will rise to the challenge to be greater than I was a second ago. I am one of a kind and no one is like me so I must live like I am. I am blessed and highly favoured. I am unbreakable. What belongs to me will find me. I speak life to the greatness that is in me.

_____

CHAPTER 10

Be You Love You Because Everyone Else is Taken

BE YOU LOVE YOU

Love is from the soul of God that gives life to who you are to be. Once you truly understand that you have the power of God in you to Be you then you will live to outlast this life.

Can a lion be at tiger? Many people talk about the lion being the king of the jungle but I am not too sure because there is something about being a tiger that I like that at lion don't have. Have ever really taken time to look at the tiger? Well, I have and the lion likes to take care of the pride, but the tiger likes to take care of himself and hunts alone, a lot more. The tiger is a lot faster than the lion and I am not telling you to become at tiger lover, but what I would tell is that the tiger knows who he is.

BE YOU LOVE YOU

      Everyone wants to be a lion, but the truth is that not everyone can be a lion and that doesn't make you be the king that you are. We are not the same and it's not just being the lion that makes you amazing or powerful or the king that you are. Everyone can be a king or queen regardless of who you are.

      Today is your day to really ask yourself are you really being who you are or are you being someone that people say or think you are? The truth is we have become so programmed that we are really lost to know who we are, right down to what we want.

      Yes, we go out with our friends for a meal and just say I'll have what they are having and never really look at the menu. It may sound simple but it has become normal for many people because it could take up at little more time to making others uncomfortable and may put the spotlight on you.   If you are thinking to yourself right now about the times that you have just let things pass because you don't want to be a bother or trouble for others, then you better start thinking about are you really living the life that you want. Are you being who you are created to be.

      God has taken time to create you in a specific way and a specific time. You must be strong and believe that you have something that others don't have and you will be someone that others may not be. You can be the first in your family to be or to do. I can tell you that when I said that I was going to be a motivational speaker that some friends and family laughed. I was the first to be an author in my family, but not the last because someone has to be. You can be who you want to be and not let anyone or anything stop you. This is your only chance to live this life.

Many times, we run after loving other people even more than we love ourselves and we lose ourself. To really know how to love we must first love God as He loves us and give ourself the love that He gives us. Self-care is important and should never be overlooked. Stop waiting and putting it off saying when I get time I will and never get to it. You are at priority. Life is nothing without you. The job is nothing with you. If you're sick, the job will go on and they will find someone else to do the job.

I had to learn this the hard way. In the pandemic, I was looking after everyone and doing my best to help others. I became very sick with covid and this has changed my life. I have never really been sick my whole life. I was at home locked away in my room. I felt like I was dying. When it passed, I was not the same and I promised myself I would put my health first.

BE YOU LOVE YOU

<u>Affirmation</u>

****

If God say I can then I will. With God I know I can do all things. I can make it through anything. There is no mountain too high or valley too low that I cannot get through. I was born to be amazing so I will be amazing. I will walk by faith to know that everything I ask for will come to past. I will love me for who I am and what I am. My dreams will come true. I will follow them with my heart. I will bring more joy and peace into this world.

CHAPTER 11
Unconditional Love is Everything, It Serves a Greater Purpose

**Since we receive God's unconditional love, it is up to us to love unconditionally too, and this means being able to receive.
- Cathy Grant**

What is love? This is one of the greatest misunderstandings of life. This is where the enemy (evil) lives and has a full-time job to make sure that every human never really understands it or ever discovers it. It is the whole sole purpose that no one will ever get the understanding or ever see the light of the power of true love.

You might think, ok, where am I going with this, but as you have nearly come to the end of this book you must feel or see some things that you need to add to your life to help you to live your best life every day, but nothing really matters without love. Love is everything and everything is love. Love will outlast you.

The type of love I want you to think about is one where you only want to be a blessing to everyone you meet with nothing in return but the love that you give. It is love that saved me and awakened me to live this life and it's because I found that love was in me and everyone one of us as humans. Many people use the words I love you, but never really do love because they are looking for something in return.

Love is the highest and most powerful energy that is in this world, once you experience it. The problem is that many will never see it or find it because it can't be seen or found. This is the love that is put in us to be the light and just be one that others want to be like because they feel it in us and can hear it. It is the light of the world and the healing of every pain that we go through.

I remember after been engaged to be married to this woman and being together for six years plus that I was ready to give my life to her forever as I thought she wanted to do the same. I could not understand why she would want to leave me or walk away after saying I love you so many times and giving me so many years. And I know that I am not the only one that has gone through this or have had a broken heart, but I want you to know that I am happy that she did. It was by far the best thing that has ever happened to me because I would not have discovered uncontestable and amazing love that I had inside

BE YOU LOVE YOU

of me for all this time that was full and overflowing.

You have it too. It has been within you, not dead. Yes, love is life. Now you must really accept this as truth to be able to unlock it. You are very important and that's why you are here. It's not to have all the pleasures that you desire alone. And yes, I know you have been thinking of all the things that you think you love and want. You might ask, how I know this, well I was just like you.

So, stop looking for love and stop fighting for love. This has already been done and love is not something that can be found. It is already in you and for you to learn to master and to understand. This is what you must learn, to earn the blessing that comes with love. Once you understand this, you will find the love comes with all the things that you are looking for: husband, wife, house, job, money, and the list can go on and on.

Yes, the love you carry is the light you carry. When you turn your light on you will soon see that everyone comes to the light. Remember that there is an equal amount of response to the love you have.

When you learn to really connect with your inner peace you will soon see that God will

BE YOU LOVE YOU

guide you into all your ways to lead you to what you need. You see, love is so much bigger than your needs that it will push you to do more for others to really experience the true power of love.

Love starts with you and the love of God that got you here. You may not want to call Him God but let's just say He is the author of love and moves in it and every second. When you speak, it flows through you and goes out to serve you. This is where your business is within you and the more it comes from. It's the greatness that is within you that you came to do more for others and not just for yourself. Love is what brings us all together. It is what holds us close. It is the only thing that can heal the pain of this world, not success, money or fame. These all come because of the love you give.

BE YOU LOVE YOU

****

*Love is the strongest
force the world possesses, and yet it is
the humblest imaginable.
- Gandhi*

BE YOU LOVE YOU

The Author's parents
Mr Agustus and Mrs Ismay Allen

BE YOU LOVE YOU

The Author's Family

BE YOU LOVE YOU

ACKNOWLEDMENTS

First of all, I want to tell you it's because of my best Jesus that I made it this far. My wife, Evette, for standing by me that last 12 years from homelessness. My family, brothers, Ian, Crenston, Noel, Glenbert, sisters, Beverly Roastta, Tannasha. My mom and dad, Aguesta Isamy Allen. My teacher, Cindy Cemons. Friends, Devon, Lyndon, Kendel, Kevern, Simon, Omar Genes Farrel Basil Chambers Steve Harvey. Tricia Therese Stone, To all of my social media supporters I could not do this without you. Knockouttime Family, YouTube, Facebook, LinkedIn, Instagram, Clubhouse, Tiktok. I want to, most of all, thank all my haters for you buying this book and reading it. It is because of you that I live. To all the people came as Goliath's that did not believe in me and always have something bad two say about me. Thank you is because of you that I keep going.

BE YOU LOVE YOU

ABOUT THE AUTHOR

GERSHOM ALLEN is one of the top international motivational Speakers, in the world, that has been blessing thousands of peoples' lives with his story and inspiring them to live their best life and to help them to come out of dark places of their life. He was homeless in London and he was able to rise above. He loves God and his family. He is married to his wife, Evette, and he has two children, Eshani and Josiah. He is from the island of Montserrat that had an active volcano in 1995. He has spoken in churches, schools, colleges, events, universities and prisons. He loves the seaside and nature a lot. This is where he gets most of his inspiration from. He is now a published Author of five books. He has worked with people with mental illness and challenging behaviour for ten years. He loves to help people be who they are called to be. He believes that every human that is here on the planet has a greater purpose if they choose to find it. From collage drop out to back to college and university. He loves God and He is greatest inspiration.

BE YOU LOVE YOU

AUTHOR PRAYER FOR YOU

Dear God,

I love you. Help me to trust you more than I trust myself. Help me to know that you know what is best for me. Let me not take your love for granted. Teach me to focus totally on me first so I can love me the way you love me.

Help me to Be Me, Love Me.

In your name
Amen

BE YOU LOVE YOU

"FOR I KNOW THE PLANS I HAVE FOR YOU,"
Declares The Lord.
"PLANS TO PROSPER YOU AND
NOT TO HARM YOU, PLANS
TO GIVE YOU HOPE AND
A FUTURE."

Jeremiah 29:11

BE YOU LOVE YOU

BE YOU LOVE YOU WITH ALL OF YOU.

BE YOU LOVE YOU

The end.

BE YOU LOVE YOU

NOTES

BE YOU LOVE YOU

NOTES

BE YOU LOVE YOU

NOTES